Alex Le

An educational fiction stor̶̶̶̶
learns to sail a dinghy saib̶̶ ̶̶̶ ̶̶̶̶̶ ̶ ̶̶̶̶̶̶̶̶̶ and witty
teacher.

Dedication

This story is dedicated to kids. Learn, be curious, discover, and embark on bold adventures.

Acknowledgments

Thanks to Tina Schweiger for the intense dedication to the graphics: getting the sail angles right, the wind direction right, the look on Alex's face, and Dinghy's smile and eyes.

Thanks to Lauren Zykorie for the tireless editing and wonderful support and to Leslie McCulloch for the additional editing.

Thanks to my daughter, Alexandra, for providing the inspiration to write the story while stuck on the remote pacific island of Vava'u in Tonga. And thanks to Shane and Helen Walker for hosting us at the Tonga Beach Resort on Vava'U.

Written by:
Grant Headifen
Global Director of Education
NauticEd

Illustrated by:
Tina Schweiger

Published by:
NauticEd

Copyright © Grant Headifen 2018

ISBN-13: 978-0-9852474-7-8

TABLE OF CONTENTS

ALEX LEARNS TO SAIL

Chapter 1 - Happy Birthday

"A sailboat," yelped Alex with glee as he uncovered his eyes and gazed upon a shiny small sailboat, a dinghy, lying in the dark beach shed.

Alex's dad was happily standing next to him with his arm over Alex's shoulder. "Happy Birthday, son," he said. "He's all yours now."

Alex could not believe his eyes. Ever since they had moved to the beach the month before, he had sat on the balcony and watched the other kids in the beach village sail their dinghies back and forth in front of his house. Alex wasn't sure if he could do it. Sailing looked awfully difficult. There were lots of ropes on the boat and trying to figure out the sail and how the dinghies moved with the wind seemed impossible. It was a long way from Alex's inner-city skateboarding days. Still, he had continued to watch with amazement, desperate to give sailing a try.

One day, a week earlier, one of the neighborhood boys had befriended Alex and asked if Alex wanted to take his dinghy out for a sail. But Alex shyly declined, embarrassed that he did not know how to sail. For the rest of that day, he felt depressed and silently vowed that he would do something about it. But how?

And now, on his twelfth birthday, here stood his very own sailboat. The dinghy had two eyes and a mouth painted on its front. It was shiny and very beautiful - the best birthday gift ever!

Still, Alex was anxious. He was not sure he could learn how to sail it. Alex looked up at his father and asked, nodding his head towards the beach, "Do you think I will be good enough in front of the other boys and girls out there?"

Alex's father gave a little "humph" as he always did when Alex would question his own confidence. "Don't worry, Son. You'll be the best. This was my dinghy when I was a boy and it was the very same dinghy that led me to a gold medal in the Junior Olympics 30 years ago."

"Really?" said Alex with excitement, "but it looks so new."

"Oh, Dinghy tends to take care of himself," chuckled Alex's

father. Then he changed the topic and said, "Come on Son, let's get Dinghy down to the water where he loves it."

Alex thought it was strange that his father was referring to the boat as if it were human. It was early in the morning and none of the kids were out yet, so Alex was keen to get going so he would not embarrass himself in front of anyone else.

He and his dad loaded up the dinghy with all the gear and headed off to the beach. When they arrived, they laid out all the gear. Then surprisingly, Alex's father said, "Okay Son, I'll see you later," and he turned to walk away.

Feeling and looking confused, Alex said, "Wait, Dad! I don't know what to do."

"Don't worry, Son. Dinghy will help you," he replied. Alex's father smiled and promptly walked back to the house where he snuck out to the balcony, sat in his favorite sun-chair, and watched from above. He had the biggest smile on his face ever.

Chapter 2 - Who's There?

Alex was feeling completely overwhelmed with the tasks ahead of him. First, he had to assemble the boat and then, figure out how he was going to sail the boat by himself? He started feeling scared and rather disappointed that his father had left him.

There in front of him on the beach lay the dinghy and all the gear. He didn't even know the names of the stuff. There were two poles, a sail, lots of ropes, some pulleys, two boards, a stick, and a life vest.

Still, he was determined to not to embarrass himself in front of the other kids. Looking at the big long pole, he figured it must go on the boat somewhere. He picked it up and as he swung it around, it bumped into the dinghy.

"OUCH!" yelled someone.

Alex looked around and couldn't see anyone. "Who's there?" he said, wondering if he imagined the noise.

"It's me, Dinghy," came a voice. Alex looked around again and still did not see anyone.

Thinking it must be his father hiding playfully on the other side of the dinghy, Alex ran around to the other side. No one was there. "Who's playing games on me?" questioned Alex in a frightened voice.

"Don't be afraid, Alex," said the voice reassuringly, "it's me,

Dinghy."

"What? Who? Where?" stammered Alex, now just totally confused.

"Alex, look at me. I'm the dinghy."

Alex was in shock. He was looking at the dinghy, its painted-on eyes and mouth were moving! But they weren't really painted on. As he looked closer, they seemed to be part of the boat. Alex looked around to see if anyone was watching, but still, no one else was on the beach. Alex replied in a quivering voice, "Y-y-y-you're real? I m-m-m-mean y-y-you're alive? Y-y-y-you can talk?"

The dinghy replied "I speak nineteen languages. Parlez vous Francais? Hablas Espanol? Você fala português? Sprichst du Deutsch? E korero ana koe i te reo Maori?"

"B-b-but you're a dinghy," said Alex still stunned.

"Of course I'm a dinghy. Do I look like anything else?" smiled the dinghy.

Alex just couldn't believe what he was seeing. He began pinching himself to see if this had all been a dream. "Do you have a name?"

"My name is Dinghy, proud to make your acquaintance" spoke Dinghy with the most refined English accent.

"Well, I'm jolly proud to make your acquaintance too," said Alex trying to mimic the accent. They both began to laugh.

7

Alex began firing off a ton of questions: "Where are you from? I mean, I really don't understand. You know my father? How did you get here? You speak nineteen languages? How do you do that? Dad said you and he won the junior Olympics? Did you teach my dad to sail?"

"Hold on, hold on, Alex," said Dinghy. "Yes, your father and I had quite the race back then. It was awesome. We worked as a team training for months and months. Your father didn't think we could even beat the local time trials, but we trained together and won the gold medal by a split second! Since then, I've been traveling around to many places in the world. I've raced in lots of regattas, but never managed to collect a gold medal since then. But when your father mailed me last month that you were coming of age, I said I'd love to come and meet you. So ... here I am."

"You came to meet ME? W-w-w-would you teach me to sail?" asked Alex.

"If you want to learn, I'd be honored to teach your father's son," announced Dinghy, again putting on the funny upper class English accent.

"Oh yes, please!" exclaimed Alex, jumping excitedly.

Chapter 3 - Help From A Strange New Friend

"First," said Dinghy, "the big pole that you whacked me with is called the mast. It holds up the sail. Please do try to be careful with my equipment - it takes me a long time to polish out those scratches. And besides, I go faster when I'm happy, shiny, and looking new."

"Sorry," said Alex making a pact with himself to treat Dinghy with respect. After all, he was almost human.

"That's OK. Apology accepted. Now, let's get me rigged properly. I'll teach you the names of each part and show you where it goes."

Pretend you are Dinghy and help Alex. Teach Alex the names of the parts using the picture of Dinghy assembled on the next page. The answer page is in the glossary at the end of this book under "Names of Parts".

Chapter 4 - The Basics

After a little while, Alex could recite all the names of Dinghy's parts. Dinghy was very proud of Alex. Now Dinghy could give Alex clear instructions on what to do out on the water without having to describe each piece of gear. He would simply use the name of each part and Alex would know exactly what he was talking about.

Next, Dinghy taught Alex how to assemble all the newly named parts onto his hull. But first, he made sure that Alex turned him around to face into the wind direction while he was being assembled.

"Why do you want to face into the wind?" asked Alex.

"It's a safety thing when rigging, Alex," said Dinghy. "You should always assemble me while I am facing into the wind. That way, my boom and sail will always fly smoothly and downwind from my mast. It is much more stable."

Alex was beginning to realize that there was a lot of safety lessons he needed to learn before he could be a really good sailor.

Dinghy however, was feeling much more like himself now that he was rigged.

"Good job, Alex. Now we're properly rigged. Are you getting excited?" Dinghy himself was smiling, itching to feel the wind in his sails and the splash of the water against his hull.

Alex started skipping around in the sand. This was the best birthday ever and it was still early in the day.

Dinghy was chuckling away. Alex's little skips mimicked his fathers all those years ago when they took the Gold.

"First Alex, I want you to know we're going to need to act as a real two-person team. I can't move any parts of my gear so I'm relying on you to do that for me."

"Dinghy? Do you think we could win the gold too?" asked Alex.

"Easy as we go, Alex. Today I want to teach you the basics. Then we'll get the finer points more exact later. All we want to do today is to learn about how my controls make me go

through the water and how I react with the wind. We'll con-
centrate on winning the Gold tomorrow, alright?" laughed
Dinghy.

Alex nodded. He had got the point. Basics first. Still, he was
eager to learn everything he could. He quickly imagined a
big gold medal hanging around his neck.

"Let's learn about the mainsheet and how it controls the sail,"
stated Dinghy, interrupting Alex's daydream.

"The mainsheet is attached to the boom and it lets the boom
out and pulls it in. Since the sail is attached to the boom,
you'll control the angle of the sail to the wind letting out or
pulling in on the mainsheet," explained Dinghy.

"But why do we do that?" Alex asked.

"Well, we adjust the sail angle to the wind so that the sail
catches the wind in the most efficient manner. Imagine you
and your dad trying to hold a big tarpaulin against a strong
wind. It would just push you both over, right? But if you held
the tarpaulin just at one end, it would flap and would be easy
to hold, right? So the force on the tarpaulin is dependent on
the angle that it is held to the wind."

Again, Alex nodded.

Dinghy continued, "For me to move as fast as possible
through the water, you and I will work together to capture
the force of the wind at the most efficient angle. We'll adjust
the mainsheet and turn me towards or away from the wind,
depending on the angle we are heading."

"Oh yes," said Alex, "I get it! We change the angle of the sail with the mainsheet so that it best catches the wind. But which is the best angle?"

"It's just best to experience that when we get on the water so you can see and feel it for yourself. Okay? For now, I'll just tell you what I expect you to do when we get out there. I promise you'll understand all the reasons later. For now, I just want you to get this: there are five basic positions of the sail."

Dinghy took a big breath, concentrated and then blew hard into the sand. A picture magically appeared. Alex squealed with excitement when he saw the picture Dinghy had drawn.

Chapter 5 - The Wind

"Whoa! How'd you do that?" asked Alex in astonishment.

"Oh, I've just done it a few thousand times." In reality, Dinghy had practiced this probably over ten-thousand times before he'd gotten it right. It was his best trick and he was proud of it.

"It shows that as the dinghy angle changes to the wind, the set of the sail must also change. Do you see how the sail is set differently for each direction?"

"Yes, I think so," said Alex, a little unsure. He then began pointing to each dinghy while describing what he thought the magical image in the sand was trying to say. "When we are heading close to the wind direction, I should have the sail all the way in tight. When we're heading a little up-wind, but mostly across the wind, the sail should be out a bit. When we are heading directly across the wind, I should have the sails out quite a bit. If we're heading downwind a bit, but still sort of across the wind, the sail should be out almost all the way, and if we're heading downwind, the sails should be all the way out. And I'm guessing that I should use the mainsheet to pull the sail in or let it out - right Dinghy?"

"Couldn't have said it better myself," said Dinghy

Alex studied the diagram and memorized it. He knew it was going to come in handy later. He did not want to disappoint Dinghy when they were out on the water. One of the ways he remembered it was that the closer he would head to the direction of the wind, the tighter he must pull in the sail.

Now look at the diagram Dinghy created. Remember how much to let the sails out depending on Dinghy's angle to the wind.

Chapter 6 - Points of Sail

Dinghy blew again and words appeared. "Here is the name for each direction, Alex."

"Those are some funny names," said Alex trying his best again to memorize them. He gave Dinghy his ideas to remember the names:

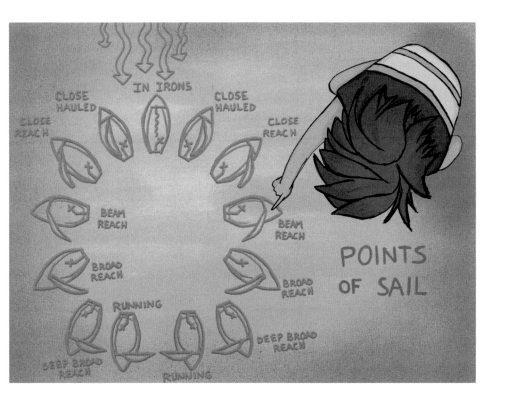

He "REACHES" across the table to steal food from his sister's plate when she is not looking. So when he points across the wind, he is reaching.

"CLOSE" must mean closer to where the wind is coming

from. So a "CLOSE REACH" must be when the dinghy is pointing a bit more upwind than a reach.

"BROAD" means wide and big so that must be when the dinghy is pointing wider away from the wind than a reach.

"DEEP BROAD" is bigger than broad so that must be pointing almost all the way down wind.

"RUN" is when he ran away from the bullies at his old school, so that means when the dinghy is running away from the wind."

A haul is when you're pulling something uphill, so a "CLOSE HAUL" means when the dinghy is pointing closest to the wind, (but perhaps a little bit away from the wind so that the sails can fill).

Dinghy just nodded his eyes in agreement, approving of Alex's mnemonics.

Chapter 7 - Review

Try for yourself. Look at the diagram Dinghy drew, and help Alex with the name of each point-of-sail for each boat. The answer sheet is in the glossary at the end of this book under "Points of Sail".

CLOSE HAULED   CLOSE REACH   BEAM REACH   CLOSE REACH   CLOSE HAULED   BEAM REACH

RUNNING   BROAD REACH   IN IRONS   DEEP BROAD REACH   BROAD REACH   RUNNING   DEEP BROAD REACH

Chapter 8 - Getting Started

Dinghy noticed that the breeze had picked up to a steady 10 knots - perfect for learning. He spun his eyes around towards Alex and announced, "The wind is blowing at a nice 10 knots. Let's get going. Make sure the mainsheet is let out before putting me into the water, otherwise I might take off without you, or worse yet, capsize! I'm not ready to get completely wet this early in the morning. Also watch out for your head on the boom. One reason it's called a boom is that it is the same sound it makes if it hits you in the head. It's apparently not very pleasant, at least, that's what all the humans complain about."

Alex let out the mainsheet a little then fired a bunch of questions at Dinghy, "What's a knot? And what's the best wind speed? And how do you know it's 10 knots?"

"Well," Dinghy started with a new voice that sounded like a TV documentary commentator. Overly long eyebrows grew over his eyes and his hull color changed to something that looked like a tweed jacket. "Sailing is rich with historical and hysterical nautical terms. In olden times, sailors measured how fast they were sailing by tossing the end of a rope overboard with an attached floating board and lots of knots tied along its length. Then they would count the number of knots on a rope that would pay out before a sand timer ran out. Thus, speed was measured in 'knots' and it still is today."

Dinghy then changed back to looking more like himself. "When you walk, you go about three knots. Running is about seven knots. When you sprint as fast as you can you're going about 15 knots. Between five and ten knots of wind speed is about the best for learning. The boat is maneuverable and responds well to the controls. When the wind is above ten knots, the waves get a little bumpy and it's hard to control the lines. When it gets to 15 knots, you should be an expert before you go sailing, and anything above 20 knots can be quite dangerous. I can tell it's about ten knots because the wind is rippling the water into little waves about two or three human hands high but the waves are not yet breaking into little white caps. That happens at about 12 knots."

Alex was grateful for the information and safety tip. Then he tightened the buckles on his life-vest and began pushing Dinghy into the water.

Dinghy wasn't budging. "Hold your horses, Alex. One thing

to always think about first is to know where the wind is coming from so you can start controlling the sails as we head out."

Alex looked up. He could feel the wind, but couldn't figure out how Dinghy knew which direction it was coming from. Dinghy noticed the confused look on Alex's face.

"The wind is blowing directly onto the shore. You can tell by turning your head. When you hear the wind in both ears, the wind is coming from where you are looking. Also, look at the seagulls over there above the cliff. See them hovering? Which ever direction they are looking when hovering, that is the direction the wind is coming from. See the smoke coming out of that house to your left? See the direction the smoke is going? Can you see the flag above the yacht clubhouse? They show you the direction of the wind. See the little waves on the bay? The wind is at right angle to the waves. See the birds on the power line up there? Birds always point their faces into the wind when they sit on power lines."

"Wow! Dinghy, you're really observant. You noticed all those things in just a few seconds," said Alex.

"Yup!" replied Dinghy. "When you've been sailing for a while you don't even have to think about it. You see all those things and more everywhere you go, even when you're not sailing."

Alex slowly turned around listening to hear when the wind would sound in both ears. Then he looked at all the other signs Dinghy had described and instantly, a whole new world opened up to him. The one thing that amazed him the most was the birds pointing into wind as they sat on the power lines. That was funny, he thought.

Dinghy interrupted Alex's thoughts, "And Alex, there's one more thing that is completely obvious about the wind direction right in front of you."

Alex looked around seeing the birds, the smoke, the flags, and the water that Dinghy had told him about, but could not see anything else that might indicate the wind direction.

"Alex, loosen the mainsheet all the way out. When the sail is loose, it will always blow down wind," Dinghy instructed.

Alex flicked the mainsheet out of its cleat and saw how the sail just started flapping exactly away from the direction of the wind. "Wow, he thought to himself, Dinghy is pretty clever."

Dinghy was feeling confident that they would be good team mates. "Now, we're almost ready. But first, we need to plan our direction to sail off the beach. Since the wind is blowing on shore, let's head out towards that island that looks like a volcano over there," said Dinghy.

"It is a volcano, but why should we head in that direction?" asked Alex.

"Well, I'm guessing you already know that a sailboat can't sail directly into the wind. But we're pretty good at sailing close to where the wind is coming from. If you look at an old clock and pretend the wind is coming from 12 o'clock, I can aim anywhere from about two o'clock all the way around to about ten o'clock".

"But two o'clock, Dinghy, that's still sort of into the wind, isn't it? How can we do that?"

"Get me into the water, Alex, and I'll show you," smiled Dinghy, knowing that this was the strangest thing that humans had to grasp when they first begin to learn how to sail.

That was the invitation Alex was looking for. Alex looked at Dinghy, gave him a thumbs up, and started again pushing Dinghy again into the water. But Dinghy still wasn't moving.

"Pull me into the water with the painter line rather than pushing me. You'll find it a lot easier," said Dinghy.

Alex ran around to the front of Dinghy, grabbed the line attached to the front of him and began pulling him into the water. Dinghy was right ... it was much easier.

When Dinghy and Alex were in about one foot of water, Dinghy told Alex to point him towards the volcano that was at about two o'clock away from the wind direction and then to step around to the left side of Dinghy on the upwind side of him. Dinghy rolled a little to his side and lowered his gunwale where Alex was standing. "Climb aboard," he invited.

Alex had never been more excited. Any anxiety left over from the invitation he'd received from that boy to go sailing last week was gone. Alex trusted Dinghy and he was excited as… as … well he just didn't know what to compare his excitement against so he just left it as excited as… and leapt aboard yelling, "Aye-Aye Captain." Dinghy gave a little chuckle. He'd taught dozens of kids after Alex's father over the years, but Alex was turning out to be one of the most excitable and enjoyable boys ever.

"Now grab on to the tiller and hold it steady in the center of my hull," directed Dinghy.

Alex obeyed and reached out for the tiller with his right hand. Alex noticed that Dinghy was just bobbing in the water and his sail was just flapping. Alex knew what to do. He was pointed towards the volcano and the wind was to the left of the front of Dinghy.

From the diagram Dinghy had blown in the sand, Alex remembered he was on a close haul – almost into the wind. He reached out and pulled in on the main sheet and almost immediately, Dinghy began making way through the water. Alex pulled hard on the mainsheet and Dinghy began moving faster. Alex pulled the main sheet all the way in so that the boom was almost along the centerline of Dinghy's hull.

Dinghy was moving fast now, but he was also heeling over son much that Alex was worried about tipping over. Dinghy instinctively yelled out, "Hook your feet under the straps on the floor and lean out to counter-balance the wind, Alex."

Alex did so and then Dinghy rolled himself flat.

Dinghy said, "Now push the daggerboard all the way down into the slot. The daggerboard stops me from slipping side-ways through the water from the force of the wind." Dinghy began humming then broke out in a little verse, "Sailing, sailing, sailing the ocean blue." Dinghy was happy. "Steady as she goes there, Alex," he cried out over the noise of the waves now slapping against his hull.

Alex, too, was elated. He'd never even been on a sailboat before and here he was sailing it now for the first time alone. Well, not really alone he remembered, he had his new friend Dinghy. Once again, he pinched himself to make sure this was not just a fantastic dream. He was glad that he wasn't waking up and that this was really happening. "Yippee!" he squealed.

Alex's father was still observing from the balcony above and he was the proudest father ever. He knew that Alex would be busting through some self-confidence doubts and feeling real achievement. He waved to Alex and to his oldest friend Dinghy. They didn't see him, however. Both of them were having too much fun. Still, Alex's father knew that this experience was going to change his son's life forever, as it did his, 30 years ago.

Chapter 9 - Steering and Capsizing

It was time to teach Alex how to steer, thought Dinghy. "Alex, pull the tiller ever so slightly towards you," Dinghy Instructed.

Alex puller the tiller and noticed the dinghy turning away from the volcano, more downwind Now they were sailing parallel to the beach. At the same time, Dinghy began to heel over more.

"Okay, that's enough. Now push the tiller back to the center," instructed Dinghy.

Again, Alex followed Dinghy's instructions. Almost instantly, Dinghy straightened out and was heading on a course parallel to the beach. Dinghy was still heeled over which was a bit too uncomfortable for Alex. Alex was confused about what he should be doing: let the sail out or in; turn Dinghy one way or the other; lean in or lean out; he just wasn't sure. Meantime, his friend just hummed away, challenging Alex to think for himself.

At last Alex remembered he was heading on a beam reach! The sails should be ... let out quite a bit. He reached down and flicked the mainsheet out of its cleat and let out the sail. Dinghy immediately started moving faster again and he also flattened out making Alex much more comfortable.

"Clever lad," yelled Dinghy back to Alex. I think this boy has the same knack for sailing as his father, and perhaps even more, Dinghy thought.

"Okay Alex, let's head back towards that volcano," said Dinghy.

Alex hesitated. Like a possum fixated on the headlights of an approaching car, Alex could not figure out which way to move the tiller to bring Dinghy back to heading that was towards the volcano. Frustrated, he pulled the tiller towards himself and in the direction of the volcano figuring it just must work like that. Dinghy immediately turned downwind away from the volcano, and towards the beach. He rolled hard to the left nearly tossing Alex out of the cockpit.

"DUCK YOUR HEAD," barked Dinghy in as loud a voice as he could muster and just as well, because as Alex dropped his head, the boom came swinging over dangerously fast. Then to make things worse, Dinghy began heeling over more to the left, "Alex, quickly cross to the other side."

Alex was in a real state of panic. One minute he was going along fine and the next he was rolling around in the bottom of the cockpit with ropes lying all over him and his feet in the water. He'd seen how fast the boom had come across and had heeded Dinghy's call to duck just in time. Now Dinghy was turning along the beach again but in the opposite direction and he began heeling over even more as the wind caught the sail. Alex was trying to get to the other side of the boat but Dinghy was heeling over so much that he couldn't. In another split second, Dinghy tipped over tossing Alex out of the boat into the morning chilled salt water. The mast and sail fell into the water with Dinghy lying on his side. In just a few seconds they had gone from laughing, to both being in the drink.

Alex's life-vest was holding Alex buoyant in the water, but he was still feeling the panic and he was breathing fast and hard. He became frantic thinking about Dinghy sinking which panicked him more. He was kicking his feet hard and flailing his arms. As he did this, the lines from the boat began to tangle in his arms. Things were not looking good.

"Yippeeeeee," yelled Dinghy, "Wahooo! Yeah! Now that's what I'm talking about. That was awesome! Give me some more, high five."

"What? What are you doing? We're in the water. We're capsized and stuck. You're going to sink. I'm way out here far from shore. There's no one around to save us." Alex began sobbing heavily.

"No man, we're just getting started. Welcome to the first of hundreds of capsizes. I've been over like this nine thousand two hundred and forty two times. Oh, correction nine thousand, two hundred, and forty three times now. I'm shooting for ten thousand. I think that might be a world record among us dinghies," said Dinghy in a slightly crazy voice that mimicked Jack Nicholson, a famous actor.

"So, we're not going to die?" questioned Alex in a high-pitched, serious voice.

"Don't be silly, Boy! My brother says 'If you're not living on the edge, you're taking up too much space.' And well, sometimes ya just got to go over the edge to experience it. Ya got to see where the edge really is. Today you experienced it. Wahooo! Yeah!" Dinghy sounded pumped up.

"You've got a brother?" asked Alex.

"Two. One older, one younger. And I have two sisters but

they are ships," replied Dinghy.

"Do they talk too?" asked Alex.

"All boats talk, Alex. In one sense or another. Some more than others. You've just go to listen. Although I have to admit, I'm a bit more vocal than most," chuckled Dinghy.

"Hey Alex, what's a pirate's favorite letter of the alphabet?" said Dinghy.

Alex was confused. They were tipped up in the sea and Dinghy was asking crazy questions. "Ummmm. I don't know," he hesitantly replied still confused.

"ARHRRRRRR," replied Dinghy with a gruff voice while a patch magically appeared over his eye.

Alex laughed. He'd stopped kicking and flailing and was letting the life vest hold him buoyant in the water.

Alex's father had his binoculars up to his eyes watching the events taking place. He remembered his first capsize and how he'd panicked. He bet Alex was feeling it now too. Zooming in, he saw Dinghy's mouth talking away and chuckling. "ARHRRRRR," he laughed to himself, "Dinghy is still telling that old joke all these years later." Alex's father knew that Dinghy used that joke to calm people down when they were panicking. There was also one about a sea cucumber and a mollusk but he couldn't remember the punch line.

"So, how do we get back up Dinghy?" Alex questioned.

"First, release the mainsheet, then swim around the other

side of me, then climb up onto the daggerboard."

Alex reached through the water, found the mainsheet, and unclipped it. Then, following Dinghy's instructions, he swam around and began to climb up onto the daggerboard. Almost immediately, Dinghy began to right himself.

"Now, climb up into my cockpit and bail out the water with that half cut down milk jug tied on to the foot strap".

Alex did so, and in a few moments, he announced, "Finished Dinghy. Can we get going again?"

"Time for another lesson, Alex. One day I want to get to ten thousand capsizes, but not all today. Okay?"

Alex laughed and nodded in agreement. It had been quite

traumatic and he was keen to learn how not to do it again.

"First things first, Alex. You will always be sitting on the up-wind side of the boat to use your body weight to balance the heeling force of the wind on my sails. The reason we capsized is that, as the boom came across, we needed to get you to switch sides. Otherwise your weight and the force of the wind on the sail act in unison to tip me over. So you've always got to switch sides as the boom comes across. Get it?"

Alex remembered Dinghy's command to switch sides during the crazy event, but had been more worried about saving himself so he had not obeyed as fast as he should have.

"What you fear most, you create, little grasshopper," Dinghy whispered while squinting his eyes. "You feared the boat tipping over. By not reacting, and not switching sides, you actually created your own fear - a capsize."

"It's also a real rule of life Alex. The more time you spend thinking about a bad outcome, the more likely that WILL ACTUALLY HAPPEN. And, this is a prime example to carry with you. Concentrating on capsizing will capsize you," Dinghy tutored.

Alex thought back to some things in the past that made this sound familiar. Worrying about the bullies at his last school meant that he showed more fear than the other kids, which only served to fuel the bullies to chase him more. Worrying about failing that mathematics test last month meant that he'd spent less time studying which created the low grade.

Alex looked at Dinghy and said, "You're not just a dinghy are you Dinghy?"

"Sailing has so many analogies to real life Alex. Learning here will carry farther into your business and personal life than you can possibly imagine," advised Dinghy.

Dinghy brought the topic back to sailing, "Okay, let's talk more about steering basics. Because you're always sitting opposite the sail and on the upwind side of the boat this makes it quite convenient to consistently remember which way you move the tiller to steer. If you pull the tiller towards you, I will always turn down wind and away from you. Conversely, if you push the tiller away, I will always turn upwind and towards your side of the boat. Come on, let's practice that one."

Alex got the boat moving again by pulling in on the mainsheet. Since they were pointed along the beach and heading across the wind, Alex only pulled the mainsheet in a little. Dinghy started moving nicely through the water again. The wind was on the right-hand side of Dinghy.

Alex pulled the tiller towards him a little then quickly put it back to center afraid that he'd repeat the last episode. Dinghy responded by turning downwind a little then straightening out. Now Alex pushed the tiller away from him and centered it again. Dinghy responded by turning upwind then straightening out. Alex was excited.

"Let's head back to towards the volcano," suggested Dinghy.

"But we're heading away from it now," said Alex. "How do we turn all the way around without capsizing again?"

"We're going to do what is called a 'tack.' First, let's get me sailing fast onto a close haul. Then turn me up into the wind so that I'm facing directly into the wind. Then, as we are pointing into the wind, cross over to the other side of me and then turn me downwind a bit towards the volcano."

Alex pictured this maneuver in his head and slowly pushed the tiller away. Dinghy turned upwind and as he did, Alex began pulling the mainsheet in tighter and tighter to match the sail set he'd learned on the beach. "Close haul is close to the wind and close to the wind meant having the sail pulled all the way in," remembered Alex.

Dinghy started splashing through the water fast. When they were on a close haul, Alex centered the tiller again.

Dinghy asked Alex if the traffic was all clear. "Make sure

there is no one close to us as we turn Alex. Always check for other boats before we make a turn."

Alex looked around. The area was clear. Alex pushed the tiller away again. Dinghy's sail started to flap.

"Don't worry about the sail flapping, just keep going," Dinghy cried out over the noise of the sail. Then for effect Dinghy yelled out, "TACKING".

When Dinghy's face was pointed to the wind, Alex slipped under the boom and pulled the tiller towards him so that Dinghy would now turn back towards the volcano.

Dinghy's sail filled with a "fump" sound and now they were off again speeding through the water. They were again on a close haul, but now sailing with the wind on the left-hand side of Dinghy.

Chapter 10 - Tacking and Gybing

For the next hour, Dinghy and Alex practiced steering and tacking around the bay.

Alex always made sure that the sail set was exactly as he'd learned on the beach. And he was very careful not to repeat the capsize from before, although he noticed that if he was slow at letting the sail out when they steered from a close haul to a beam reach, Dinghy would heel over a lot. Alex would then have to lean backwards out of the boat so that they would not capsize and at the same time he had to let the sail out slowly. He discovered that if he leaned back to slow, Dinghy would heel over and almost launch him out of the boat. If he let out the sail too fast, Dinghy would heel over dangerously close to a capsize on top of Alex from his own weight. It was quite precarious. All the while, Dinghy was humming all his favorite tunes, "Son of a son, son of a son, son of a son of a sailor," went one of them.

"Time for a gybe, Alex," Dinghy suddenly announced.

Alex hadn't noticed it, but they were sailing up towards a reef.

"Similar to a tack, Alex, except steer downwind so that my bum ... erh, I mean my stern, points to the wind, not my face. Move to the center of the boat as we point down wind. Watch out because the boom comes across very fast. Duck, then turn back upwind and move to the other side of the boat," Dinghy quickly instructed but he knew Alex understood. The main thing was that Alex had to duck the boom as it swung across.

Alex pulled the tiller towards him. Dinghy spun downwind. This was starting out similar to the capsize from before, but Alex concentrated on what he must do instead. When they were pointing downwind Alex centered himself in the boat and pulled the tiller towards him some more, ducking his head at the same time. The boom whooshed above his head crossing over at an alarming speed. Alex was glad he'd kept his head down. He moved across the boat and pushed the tiller away to make Dinghy sail back upwind to the opposite direction, and away from the reef. Alex tightened the mainsheet a little and Dinghy began slapping the water again.

"Yahoo!" congratulated Dinghy as he started rocking around doing a dinghy dance. "You did it. The gybe is the most dangerous maneuver and you did it perfectly, Alex. Yahoo!"

Alex looked around to see if anyone had been watching, and indeed, there was now quite a few boys and girls launching their dinghies. Alex was excited that perhaps some of them had seen him complete his gybe flawlessly.

For another hour, Dinghy and Alex tacked and gybed their hearts out. There was one capsize because Alex got his feet caught in the mainsheet and couldn't let it out in time. Other than that mishap, they worked flawlessly as a team.

The boy that offered Alex his dinghy last week whizzed past and yelled out, "Nice maneuvering, Alex!" Then he tacked around and came back on the same angle as Alex. He caught up and admired Alex's shiny dinghy, "Are you going to race in the regatta tomorrow?" he questioned.

Alex didn't know about the regatta but Dinghy yelled back

magically mimicking Alex's voice, "You bet cha."

"Great!" said the boy, "see you at 9am at the race start line."
Then he tweaked his mainsheet and pulled ahead of Alex,
then tacked away.

"Dinghy, what did you say that for? I can't compete in that
race" complained Alex.

"Why not?" asked Dinghy.

"Did you see how he caught up to me so easily? He and all
the other kids will make me come last." said Alex disappoint-
ingly.

"That's only because you don't have the sail trimmed perfectly," announced Dinghy.

Chapter 11 - Sail Trim using the Main-sheet

Alex looked up surprised. He'd been doing everything Dinghy had shown him on the beach.

- Close Haul – Sail all the way in
- Close Reach – Sail out a bit
- Reach – Sail out quite a bit
- Broad Reach – Sail out most of the way
- Deep Broad Reach – Sail out all of the way
- Run – Sail out all of the way

"What else is there?"

"Oh just a few dozen things. But let's move onto sail trim. Look at the red and green ribbons in the sail window," instructed Dinghy.

"What are they?" questioned Alex.

"They are telltales," answered Dinghy. "They tell you a tale about the even flow of wind over the sail on both sides. The red one is on my left side and the green one is on my right side. To compete well in any race, the sail has to be perfectly trimmed at all times. This means that the airflow over the sails must be smooth. But since we can't see the air, we rely on the telltales to tell us. When both telltales are flowing back smoothly we know the air must be smooth. Get it?"

"Well sort of. If the air flows smoothly over the sail, the telltales will flying straight back. Does that mean if the telltales are flapping and flopping up and down that the air is not smooth?" asked Alex.

"Exactement!" said Dinghy excitedly in a funny French accent. "Erh I mean – exactly."

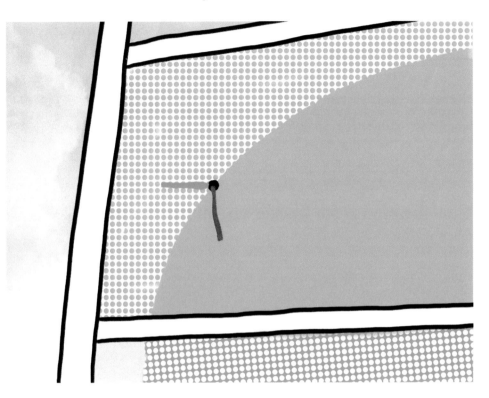

"And even better than that, by having one ribbon on each side we can tell if one side has smooth air flow while the other side has turbulent air flow. Remember both sides must have smooth air flow. The golden rule is: if the telltale closest to you is flapping then pull in the boom. If the telltale furthest from you is flapping then let out the boom," said Dinghy.

"I'm struggling to understand," hesitated Alex.

"Let's see it in real action. Turn us to a close haul, back towards the reef over there and then hold a steady course."

Alex did as instructed. The wind was coming from over the left-hand side of the boat. By now he was an expert at maneuvering Dinghy. Alex then adjusted the sails so that they were at the best setting, or so he thought.

"Now take a quick peak at the telltales. What do you see?" asked Dinghy.

"I see the red ribbon hanging down and the green one flowing back smoothly," announced Alex.

"And what does that tell you?" asked Dinghy.

"That the wind is not flowing smooth on the red telltale," said Alex.

"And?" asked Dinghy, making Alex think all this through.

"That the sail is not perfectly trimmed," continued Alex.

"And?" continued Dinghy.

"Well I must adjust the boom one way. But I don't know which way," said Alex.

"Which side is the red ribbon on?" Dinghy questioned further.

"My side," said Alex.

"So to move the boom towards the unsmooth fluttering ribbon you would do what?" questioned Dinghy.

"Pull the boom towards me," said Alex a bit unsure.

"Is that your final answer?" smiled Dinghy.

Alex looked up at the sails and went through the test again. Move the boom towards the fluttering ribbon. The red ribbon was not flowing smoothly and the red ribbon was on his side of the sail.

Alex started pulling in the mainsheet intently watching the telltales now. The formula worked - feed the boom in the direction of the flapping ribbon. Both telltales were now streaming evenly backwards. But then as quickly as that happened the red started to flutter and fall down. Alex pulled the mainsheet again to get the red ribbon flying. He didn't know what was happening. He was so intent on watching the telltales that he didn't notice that he and Dinghy were turning dangerously into another boat that was anchored in the bay.

"ALEX... LOOKOUT!" loudly but still calmly announced Dinghy.

Alex looked down from the telltales, saw the boat and immediately pulled the tiller towards him to turn away from the boat just it time. But as they passed the boat, it shadowed the wind from Dinghy's sails and with Alex's weight on the upwind side they dangerously tipped over towards the wind so that Alex nearly fell out. Alex moved his weight into Dinghy's cockpit quickly to counterbalance the tipping. Then, worse yet, as they came out from behind the boat, a gust blew through and slammed into Dinghy's sails. Now, with Alex's weight inboard, there was nothing to stop them from being tossed into the water, again. Dinghy went over first and Alex was tossed onto Dinghy's sail.

Alex's feet were tangled in the mainsheet. With Alex's weight on the sail, the sail started to sink and Dinghy rolled completely over upside down. Alex's head was dragged under the water.

Alex's Dad on the balcony leapt up out of his chair jamming the binoculars against his eyes. Things were not looking good. When he saw Alex's head go under the water he began running down stairs but already calculating that even if he was an Olympic swimmer, he could not swim the distance out to Dinghy in time. He could only hope that Dinghy could still do his magic trick of talking under water.

Alex was panicking. He was trying to surface away from Dinghy but the mainsheet kept holding his head down under the water. The more he struggled the more air he was using up in his lungs, and already, he was feeling like he was running out of time. He reached down and tried to pull the ropes away, but in his panic he couldn't feel where to start. All he was doing was tugging and pulling, but this wasn't working and he was starting to feel faint.

Then suddenly, Alex heard something that sounded like the dolphin calls he'd heard on reruns of Jacques Cousteau's oceanographic television shows. Yet, there were words behind the high pitched whistles.

"Wirrrpp - Swim under the boat Alex. Wirrrpp. There is plenty of air in the upside down cockpit. Wirrrp!"

Alex stopped struggling and listened. There it was again.

"Wirrrpp - Don't panic, Alex. Wirrrpp. Just move back towards the boat and surface under the cockpit. Wirrrpp."

Alex used his arms and paddled himself back under the cockpit where the length of rope would let him surface. When his head popped out of the water he was gasping for air. It felt funny under the cockpit. His sound echoed and it was slightly scary but the voice was right, there was plenty of air in there.

Alex gulped some more big breaths of much needed air. Then he nearly leapt out of his skin when Dinghy's eyes and mouth appeared on the inside of the cockpit, upside down for Dinghy but right-side up looking at Alex, and smiling.

"That was close, huh? Have you heard the joke about the black and white dolphin with the short nose, big teeth and extra long dorsal fin?" asked Dinghy.

"Dinghy! Stop that! I nearly drowned!" said Alex, frowning with a surly voice.

"Oh sorry. Well anyway you can stop panicking now and slowly untangle the mainsheet from your feet," said Dinghy.

It turned out that the knot around Alex's feet was pretty simple to undo. It was just that he was panicking so much that he couldn't think to simply slip the loop off his foot before. Once untangled, he took another deep breath and swam out from underneath Dinghy. But on the way out, he used his now clearly thinking brain and released the mainsheet from its cleat.

Moving his eyes and mouth back out to the outside of the

boat, Dinghy instructed Alex to stand on the upwind edge of the upside down cockpit, grab the dagger board, and lean back. Slowly, but surely, Dinghy was righted by Alex's light but consistent weight.

Once they were back up and sailing again, Dinghy decided to add another piece of valuable advice to Alex's already expanding mind set.

"The secret to using the telltales is not to stare at them, but just check them with a quick glance about every 5 seconds. You've got to keep your eyes out of the boat. Keep looking at where you are going. This will help you hold a straight course. Let's try it again," said Dinghy.

Alex and Dinghy set out sailing another straight line and Alex adjusted the mainsheet to get both ribbons flying smoothly backwards. The wind was coming over the left side of the boat. A few times the green ribbon dipped and he let out the sail to compensate. He kept his eyes out of the boat and on the course and where he was going.

Next, they tacked around to the other direction so that the wind was coming in over the right hand side of the boat. As they tacked around, Dinghy said to lay a close reach course. This time the green ribbon was on the same side of the sail as Alex. He repeated the rule to himself, "feed the boom in the direction of the fluttering ribbon." Alex glanced at the ribbons. The red one was fluttering. Red was on the other side of the sail - away from him. Alex let the sail out a little until it began to fly straight back.

Chapter 12 - Sail Trim with the Tiller

"This is pretty cool, Dinghy. I'm sailing the wind that I can't see," said Alex.

Alex now understood a concept that many sailors would never fully understand. Dinghy was an amazingly good teacher and explained things in such simple terms. It was only 3 hours ago that Alex had been lead by his father into the beach shed with his hands over his eyes.

Dinghy was feeling the proud moment too and he knew now that Alex was going to be a great sailor.

Dinghy decided to press on and teach Alex the last concept with the ribbons: make the ribbons fly smoothly backwards by changing the direction of the boat, not by adjusting the sails. This fine point in sail trim instruction is where some kids get it and some don't. Those that do, become great sailors. Those that don't, become average sailors.

"Alex, are you still having fun?" asked Dinghy, wanting to check to make sure Alex was still in the mood to learn more.

"Are you crazy? This is the best day of my life," blurted out Alex.

"Here's another way we can get the ribbons to fly smoothly without adjusting the sails. Move the tiller a little in the direction of the fluttering ribbon for a few seconds then center it again. Let's try it out," instructed Dinghy.

Alex and Dinghy were sailing along on a reach with the wind coming over the right-hand side of Dinghy. Alex looked up at the ribbons and saw the green was fluttering. While looking out where he was going and watching out for other boats, he thought about the new rule and how to apply it. The green ribbon was on his side of the sail. The rule was to move the tiller in the direction of the fluttering ribbon. Alex pulled the tiller towards himself a little until Dinghy turned a little. Alex straightened Dinghy out on a course by centering the tiller, then he glanced at the telltales. The green one was still fluttering although less than before. Alex made one more adjustment and then saw both telltales were flying smoothly. Alex could feel and hear Dinghy going slightly faster through the water.

"Wow," said Alex, "That is awesome!"

Chapter 13 - Sailing Rules

Dinghy was happily singing a song about a ship called Calypso, the places she'd been to and the stories she told. It was a catchy tune.

Alex continued practicing either moving the tiller to the fluttering ribbon or feeding the boom to the fluttering ribbon while heading in different directions and while on different sides of the boat. The rule definitely worked in all directions. The more Alex practiced it, the more he was doing it automatically. Seemingly, it was his hand making the decisions on the tiller rather than his conscious brain - strange he thought!

Suddenly, Alex saw another dinghy heading right at them. "Dinghy! What do I do?" cried out Alex.

"STARBOARD!" Dinghy calmly and loudly hailed to the other boat.

The other dinghy instantly changed heading to miss colliding with them. The girl steering replied back, "Thanks," as they passed. She was pretty and threw a big smile at Alex.

"What was that all about?" Alex's heart was now slowing back to normal.

"Just like the road, there are traffic rules out here too," said Dinghy. "There are quite a few but I'll teach you a few basic ones now. The number one rule of the waterway is don't hit anyone else even if you are in the right."

"Oh duh, that's pretty obvious. I don't think I'll have trouble remembering that one," said Alex.

"You'd be surprised at some of the stubborn knuckleheads out here Alex. Keep your eyes peeled at all times. You're sitting up higher than me and can see other boats before me. Accidents are mostly caused by people not knowing the rules or not keeping a proper watch out. A few years back I was nearly run down by some crusty woolly faced old guy claiming I had to give way because he was bigger than me. Then another time some guy was smooching his girlfriend and not watching out. He barely missed me, but he wasn't so lucky with the reef."

"Know the rules and keep a watch out," Alex repeated.

Dinghy replied, "The other two rules I want you to know today are (1) port tack sailboats must give way to starboard tack boats and (2) a windward sailboat gives way to a leeward sailboat."

"That sounds like one of your foreign languages to me," laughed Alex.

"Agreed. But it is just something that you need to learn. Here, let me explain," said Dinghy.

Dinghy went on to explain to Alex that the port side of the boat was the same as the left side of the boat and the starboard side of the boat is the right hand side. "Port and Left have the same number of letters. The boat with the wind on its left (port) side is said to be on a 'port tack.' A boat with the wind coming over its right (starboard) side is on a 'starboard tack." And just by world wide convention and understanding, a port tack sailboat (a sailboat with wind from its left-hand side) must give way to a starboard tack sailboat a sailboat with wind from its right-hand side.

Then he explained that for two sailboats sailing on the same tack but on a collision course the sailboat that is closest to where the wind comes from must give way to the other sailboat.

Alex was beginning to get it; "That's why you yelled STARBOARD to the girl back there. Do you think she was pretty?"

"Yes she is. Now stay focused!" Dinghy admonished Alex with a wink and a smile. "Yes, she gave way because we were on a starboard tack. The wind was coming from over the right-hand (starboard) side of me. She was heading towards us and the wind was from her port (left) side. She had to give way and I was just letting her know that we held the starboard tack."

"OK so what about that boat over there?" pointed Alex. He was pointing at a boat closer to the shore but coming out towards them.

"What tack are we on?" tested Dinghy.

"Starboard," Alex recognized that the wind was coming over the starboard side of Dinghy.

"And what tack are they on?" asked Dinghy.

Alex looked and saw that their sails were on their port side.

He therefore figured since the wind always blew the sails to the other side of the boat, that the wind must be coming from their starboard too. "Starboard," Alex proclaimed.

Dinghy pushed Alex the think further. "So, we're both on starboard tack. So then who is closer to where the wind is coming from?"

"We are." Then, remembering the second rule Dinghy had announced, Alex continued, "that means we must give way to him. Right?"

"Right," said Dinghy. "We can either turn to go in behind him or tack around away from him. You decide."

Alex pulled on the tiller and took a new course aiming behind where the approaching dinghy was coming from. Alex let out the mainsail then checked the telltales. Red was fluttering so he made a minor adjustment out on the mainsheet again. Both telltales were flying backwards and Dinghy was skipping along the water.

Dinghy just smiled. He knew he was in safe hands with Alex now and it was time to take a rest. Alex had absorbed so much information and he wanted to let it sink in before the regatta tomorrow. "Let's head to the beach Alex."

Alex was anxious to tell his Dad about everything. He couldn't wait. This day was better than the best day any kid could imagine.

The beach where they launched was slightly behind and downwind from where they were. Alex pulled the tiller towards him and let out the mainsheet to go on a run. The wind was on Dinghy's right side. "We are on a starboard run," he announced to Dinghy. Dinghy just smiled.

Alex moved to the center of Dinghy's cockpit so that his own weight was not heeling Dinghy over. He checked for any traffic and prepared to gybe Dinghy over to a port tack. He pulled the tiller in again and ducked his head as the boom whipped overhead. Now he was running downwind on a port tack. The beach was slightly to port so Alex pushed the tiller away and pulled in on the mainsheet a little.

They were both surfing fast down the waves. Dinghy broke out into another song, "I am sailing, I am sailing to be near you to be free." Alex had heard it before somewhere; it was by some famous singer named Rod something or other. He was sure his Dad would know.

Alex leaned forward and raised the daggerboard to increase the speed further. Dinghy had said to him that speed was all about reducing drag in the water and since the daggerboard was only used to stop Dinghy from being pushed sideways by the wind, Alex figured that on a downwind run the daggerboard was not being used and was only creating drag.

Dinghy smiled again. Alex had done the right thing and it had proved to him that Alex was understanding all the forces on the boat by the water and by the wind. Alex was a true natural.

As they reached the shallow water, Alex pulled a pin out of the back of the rudder so that it would swing up and not drag on the bottom. The last thing he wanted to do was to hurt Dinghy. Then, at the last moment before touching the beach, Alex pushed the tiller away hard so that Dinghy was broadside to the beach. Alex let the mainsheet all the way out and Dinghy slowed to a stop. Alex stepped out of Dinghy into the water up to his knees.

Alex's father was already waiting on the beach with his mouth wide open in amazement at how Alex had executed a perfect landing without any coaching from Dinghy. "Great job Alex. I was watching you guys from the balcony. You're a natural."

"Dinghy was the hero," Alex responded.

But Dinghy interrupted, "No, it was you Alex. If you remember, I did nothing except offer a few words of wisdom. You did all the maneuvering and the work. Erh, including the capsize."

They all laughed.

Alex's father helped Alex pack up Dinghy and they wheeled him up to the beach shed where they washed him down with fresh water. Back inside his house, Alex was famished and devoured a snapper sandwich freshly made by his mom.

Chapter 14 - Race Day

The next morning, Alex awoke at 8 a.m. and levitated out of bed. He'd overslept. Probably from all the excitement yesterday. He threw on his board shorts and tee and dashed out of the room grabbing a handful of toast off his father's plate as he raced by. Alex's father didn't have a chance to defend his own breakfast as Alex screamed past, "One hour to race start. One hour to race start."

Alex raced out to the beach shed and began wheeling Dinghy out. "Wake up Dinghy. Wake up. Fifty five minutes to race start."

Dinghy had been dreaming about chasing other dinghies all night. One, in particular, he had taken a fancy to. A big smile was resting on his face as Alex dragged him out of his sleep.

In another ten minutes they were on the beach with all the gear laid out. Alex slid the sail onto the mast then lifted up the mast so that it was pointing at the sky. He placed the mast and the sail down into the mast slot on Dinghy. He attached the boom to the mast and tied the clew of the sail to the other end of the boom. He hooked up the boom vang to the boom and to the base of the mast. He attached the mainsheet to the boom and to the center of Dinghy's cockpit. He placed the rudder with tiller attached into the pins mounted on the back of Dinghy. He placed the daggerboard into its slot in Dinghy's cockpit but didn't push it down. He'd do that once they were in the water.

All the while Dinghy was singing a song;

"Sailing
Takes me away
To where I've always heard it could be
Just a dream and the wind to carry me
And soon I will be free"

Alex ran around and tightened up the downhaul on the mast and the outhaul on the boom. Alex's mom came running down to the beach with Alex's proper warm and wind re-sistant sailing clothing, a bottle of water, and some fruit in a soft zip-up cooler. "You need your proper gear and energy Alex, otherwise you'll catch your death," she said handing over the bottle and cooler. "Your Dad told me that the din-ghy can talk and that's how you learned so fast. I'm sure he meant that you listen to the wind singing in the sails. Din-ghies can't talk, you silly. Anyway, good luck."

Just then, Dinghy sang out the last verse to the song.

"And when the wind is right you can sail away
And find serenity
The canvas can do miracles
Just you wait and see
Believe me"

Alex's mom jumped back. She looked around then down at Dinghy with her mouth wide open. Dinghy gave her a big wink. Alex's mom screamed and ran away blurting out, "it sings in real words."

Alex and Dinghy didn't have too much time to laugh. It was only 20 minutes to race start and they weren't even in the water yet! All the other kids were already out practicing and getting a feel for today's wind conditions which, fortunately for Alex and Dinghy, the new dynamic duo, were the same as yesterday.

Alex loosened Dinghy's mainsheet, then ran to the front and began pulling on Dinghy's painter trying to drag him into the water. But Dinghy pulled back on Alex and said, "whoa there Alex. Let me show you the race course." Dinghy quickly blew into the sand and instantly a picture of the race course and the buoys appeared.

Dinghy quickly explained all the buoys that they would have to sail around. Then looking at Alex's flummoxed looking face, he said, "Ah don't worry boy, just follow my lead".

Alex then launched Dinghy, pointed Dinghy in a direction a little away from the wind, leapt aboard and pulled in on the mainsheet. Almost instantly, Dinghy seemed to accelerate ahead. He too was in a hurry. He still had to teach Alex how to start a race.

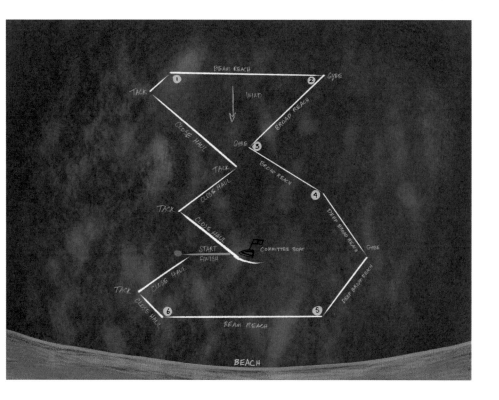

In deeper water, Alex swung down the rudder and pushed the daggerboard completely down into the slot. They were skipping along out towards the committee boat where the race was due to start in 15 minutes. Already Alex could count 14 other dinghies getting ready for the race.

Dinghy started giving instructions. He had to speak loudly over the slap-slap-slap of the waves hitting against his hull. "We've got to cross the start line as soon after the whistle blows as possible. So we have to time it right. The start line is between the committee boat, that's the boat with all the flags on it over there on the right, and a marker buoy over there on the left."

Alex's heart was racing taking in the whole scene around him; boats, race markers, people, and dinghies seemingly everywhere all heading in different directions.

Dinghy continued, "Make sure we're on a starboard tack as we start so that anyone on port tack will have to give way to us causing them to lose time. Start as close to the committee boat as possible because that will give us an up wind advantage over the others. Don't follow anyone over the start line where we are directly downwind of them, otherwise we'll be stuck in bad air coming off the back of their sail."

"Whew," Alex was thinking. "That's a lot tactical information." Still, he pictured in his mind what he must do. He figured that at about 10 seconds before the start whistle he should be about 5 boat lengths to the right of the committee boat on a starboard tack pointing on a reach towards the start line. Then, he'd sail hard at a point just leeward of the stern of the committee boat and turn up onto a close haul just as he passed it, thus crossing the start line hopefully right as the start whistle blew. He explained his tactics to Dinghy who replied that it was his favorite race start tactic. "Good, we both have the same plan," thought Alex.

Chapter 15 - The Race

"Frrrrrrrrrrrp," a whistle blew.

"That's the 5 minute warning" said Dinghy "Let's get a move on. There will be another whistle at 1 minute before the start. Let's get over to the starboard side of the committee boat."

Alex and Dinghy were on a port tack on a close haul. Alex checked his telltales to make sure they were going as fast as possible. The red was fluttering downwards. The sail was already in as tight as it could go so Alex pulled the tiller towards him to feed wind to the red telltale. Unfortunately, this made them bare away from the wind a little and away from a line to the committee boat. "We're going to be tight on time Dinghy," said Alex estimating that they were still a long way from the start line.

"Keep checking the telltales, Alex. Every 5 seconds as I said yesterday. Perhaps the wind will be on our side."

Alex glanced at the telltales and sure enough the green was now fluttering. Alex pushed the tiller away towards the green telltale side of the sail to make it fly smoothly. This put them back on course to the committee boat.

"Frrrrrrrrp," said the one minute whistle.

Alex and Dinghy were closing in on the committee boat fast now. They were still on a port tack and Alex had to watch out for other dinghies because port tack boats had to give way to starboard tacks he remembered. Dinghies were everywhere, all crossing side to side, in front and behind of Dinghy. It was exhilarating and scary. Alex didn't want one scratch on his friend, Dinghy. He ducked in behind one dinghy then had to tack over to starboard to miss another dinghy fast approaching from their right. Once it was past, Alex pulled on the tiller and tacked back to a port tack to take him to his predetermined start position ducking in behind one more dinghy.

They'd made it to the point Alex had suggested, just right of the committee boat about 5 boat lengths away.

"14 seconds," yelled Dinghy.

Alex pushed the tiller away, ducked down, let the boom swing over his head, crossed to the other side, let out the mainsheet to go on a reach, and leaned out of the boat all in one movement. He aimed just behind the committee boat. Quickly he check the telltales. Red was flapping so he let out the mainsheet a little more. Dinghy was counting, "6 – 5 – 4 – 3 – 2 – 1"

"Frrrrrrrrp," went the start whistle just as Dinghy's nose crossed right in behind the committee boat.

Alex pushed the tiller away from him and tightened up on the mainsheet as tight as it could go. He crossed the start line within two seconds after the whistle. Quickly he checked the telltales. Red was flapping, so he pushed the tiller away from him a little, then centered it again. Red was flying smoothly now.

All the other boats were on the same point as Alex. All the dinghies were going as fast as they could and the colors of the sails, all in the same row, looked exciting.

"Morning Ralph," said Dinghy to the dinghy just to their port.

"Oh, morning Dinghy. Didn't know you were in town," said the other dinghy.

"Yup, just got in yesterday from Ausy," replied Dinghy to his old friend.

"Dinghy!" yelled Alex "You're distracting me. And, where are we going by the way?"

"Oh sorry Alex. See you at the finish line Ralph. Alex, there is a big yellow buoy to windward. You've got to round that so it goes past our starboard side. The second one is way off to our starboard. We'll be on a port reach to get there."

Alex concentrated on ensuring the telltales were flying back smoothly. Since they were heading to an upwind mark, Alex wanted the boom pulled in as tight as possible. He'd make sail trim adjustments using the tiller only. Feed the tiller to the flapping telltale. If the outer telltale is flapping, push the tiller away. If the inner telltale is flapping, pull the tiller in. Alex would make very small adjustments, then center the tiller and check the telltales again every 5 seconds.

Alex and Dinghy were still on a starboard tack. No one was to their starboard direction because they had crossed the closest to the committee boat. The entire fleet was to their left.

Pretty soon though, some of the fleet began tacking over onto a port tack (wind on the left-hand side of the boat) and cutting in behind Alex and Dinghy. They would all have to do this zig-zig several times so that they could climb up on the wind to round the first mark to windward.

Dinghy thought that they would hold this course for another minute because the wind they were using here was good and steady. "We'll tack over to climb up to the windward mark in about a minute."

Alex kept sailing as high on the wind as he could, never letting the telltales fall away from flying backwards smoothly.

Alex and Dinghy tacked twice about a minute apart climbing up to the windward mark. They were back on a starboard tack, but two boys had pulled ahead of them already. Dinghy told Alex to sit further forward in the cockpit and to lean out a little more to keep Dinghy sailing flatter in the water.

Then Dinghy explained that a layline is an imaginary line from the mark extending outwards and downwind so that if they were on that line and sailed perfectly on a close haul, they could round the mark without having to tack or zig-zag again. "We'll reach that line when the mark is about the 3 o'clock position from us. As soon as we hit that line, we'll tack over onto port and sail straight for the mark."

Alex looked over his shoulder and saw that the mark was nearing the 3 o'clock position. He prepared himself to tack. About 20 seconds later, he checked that they were clear of traffic then yelled out to Dinghy, "Tacking." Alex pushed the tiller away, ducked his head, and went under the boom as it rushed overhead. Swapping hands on the tiller, he pulled the tiller in on the other side until the sail was full of wind again. He checked the telltales. Green was flapping and so he pushed the tiller away a little before centering it. Both tell-tales were flying smoothly. They were on a port tack on the layline heading right for the first mark. "Excellent," thought Alex. As long as the wind held a constant direction they were good to sail right to the mark. One of the boys ahead of him had tacked a little early and one a little later. They were about to find out who had guessed the correct layline.

Checking the telltales again, Alex could see red flapping. Oh no, this was not good. Alex had to pull the tiller towards him and bear away to a point downwind from the mark to maintain speed. He was tempted not to do it because this would mean they couldn't round the mark at this angle without tacking and losing more time.

Dinghy had felt himself slow down during Alex's hesitation. "Sail the wind Alex," Dinghy said as though he had heard

Alex's thoughts. "Sail the wind. Just keep watching the tell-tales and sail the wind."

Alex beared away a little down wind to follow the telltales. Yet again, the red began flapping. Alex was about to turn down again when Dinghy announced, "Alex, this is called a knock. It's when the wind changes to make our course to the mark worse. But it's called a lift on the other tack. Let's tack to take the advantage."

Alex pushed the tiller away and they tacked over. The two other boys kept sailing on their port tack hoping the wind would change back.

"Let's over-stand the layline a little since the wind seems to be veering a little," suggested Dinghy.

Alex didn't know what that meant but placed his trust in Dinghy.

Dinghy continued, "Wait till the mark is about the 3:30 clock position this time. The wind is changing in a clockwise direction. That will put us to the mark nicely."

Fifteen seconds later Alex figured the mark was at the 3:30 position and he tacked around to have another go at reaching the mark. As they came about, the mark was slightly downwind of their close haul heading.

"Don't be tempted to aim for the mark," Dinghy yelled. "Stay good on your close haul." Dinghy didn't want to lose any ground if the wind veered again. Which it did five seconds later. As Alex adjusted his heading to match they were now pointed ever so slightly above the mark. "Perfect," cheered

Dinghy.

The other two boys who had climbed ahead of them before were now doing their second tacks because they missed Dinghy's calculation of the wind veering. They passed behind Alex and Dinghy just as they rounded the mark.

Alex saw the next mark off to the starboard. He pulled the tiller in and set the sails for a reach. After centering the tiller on course for mark number two, he adjusted the mainsail out to match the green flapping telltale.

"Aim to the windward of the mark Alex, not right at the mark. Remember we will get some downwind side slip from the boat being pushed sideways by the wind."

Alex pushed the tiller away a little, centered it, and pulled in the mainsheet.

Alex looked behind him and saw the same pretty girl that had flashed him a smile yesterday round the first mark. She had just barely beat out the two boys who would have beaten him to the first mark had it not been for Dinghy's wind-reading expertise. She was coming on strong and catching up fast.

Mark number two was about fifty meters away and Dinghy instructed Alex that at the mark they would need to do a high speed gybe, followed by a broad reach on starboard to mark three. Alex wasn't too keen on gybes because that was the one that capsized him yesterday. At mark two, Alex pulled the tiller in hard, moved to the center of Dinghy as the boom came whooshing overhead, swapped hands on the tiller, and pulled the tiller in until he lay a course to mark three ahead on a broad reach on a starboard tack. He let out the mainsheet almost all of the way and then checked the telltales. Red was flapping down so he let out the mainsheet a little more.

The girl and two boys were right there in behind him followed by two more boys and two more girls 20-30 meters back.

"Alex, let off on the boom vang, move your weight backwards, and let out a little on the mainsheet. This will allow the sail to curve more and catch more wind. Your weight backwards will allow my front to come up giving less drag."

One of the boys was dropping back but the girl and the other boy were creeping up steadily. "If he's going to pass you, make sure it is on the downwind side. You don't want him steeling your wind if he gets above you," said Dinghy.

Alex watched the boy come right up behind him and then make a break to come up on the windward side of Dinghy. Alex pushed the tiller away a little then centered it. Dinghy was aiming a little higher. The boy tried again but Alex held him off again. Frustrated the boy turned left and went down wind of Alex.

There was nothing Alex could do except watch the boy begin to pass him and Dinghy. But that was about all the boy could do. The boy could not completely pass them because each time his sail got in the wind shadow of Dinghy's sail, he would slow down. Alex and Dinghy didn't loose any further ground to the boy. The girl was following in right behind the boy and this was going to make it difficult at the next mark which was another gybe on to a port tack. Alex and Dinghy wouldn't be able to do the maneuver until the boy and girl had completed theirs. Still the tactic had prevented the boy and girl from gaining more ground. Their boats were rigged to handle broad reaches better than Dinghy so Alex and Dinghy were going to lose this leg of the race and Dinghy was hoping his tactics on the final reach and windward legs would give them the advantage. Dinghy told Alex to gybe as soon as possible after the others.

At mark three, the boy and girl gybed away leaving the way open for Alex and Dinghy to gybe around onto a port tack. To get to mark four was also a broad reach but this time on port (with the wind over the left-hand side of the boat). Dinghy told Alex to sail across on a reach a little until the boy who was now in the lead was in the shadow of Dinghy's sail, then to turn downwind and follow in behind the two leaders.

Four other dinghies were also rounding mark three just behind them and Dinghy was concerned about getting in their shadows. Although Dinghy and Alex could not pull ahead of the leading boy and girl, they lost little ground because of Dinghy's shadowing tactic. This also allowed the other four dinghies to gain ground. So as they approached mark four there were now seven dinghies including Dinghy all within seven seconds of each other.

Alex was becoming quite nervous, "It's getting really messy Dinghy and I don't know what to do."

"Sail the wind Alex. Sail the wind."

The mark four maneuver was going to be interesting because mark five was directly down wind of mark four. Everyone was on a port tack as they approached. This meant that as they came past mark four they could decide to gybe around onto a starboard tack and go straight for mark five or let out the sail and stay on a port tack and gybe around later.

The leading boy elected to gybe to get away from Alex and the girl's shadowing tactics. But he was so intent on looking backwards at Alex and the girl that he let the wind capture the sail before he could center himself in the boat. He capsized just after he rounded the mark. The girl and Alex both had to swing wide around to get clear water. Two other dinghies from behind, a boy and a girl, gybed over and picked their way through a gap between the mark and the capsized boy. This now put the girl leading, with Alex right behind her and the other girl and the boy sailing on the opposite tack off to their right. Another girl and boy were right behind Alex. And now, to make it worse, a sudden gust of wind from behind allowed all those to capture that wind first. They picked up speed and now six dinghies were blasting their way on a deep broad reach downwind towards mark number five. Two on starboard and four of them on port.

Suddenly the girl gybed onto starboard.

"Follow her Alex. Follow her," Dinghy announced.

Alex duplicated the girl's gybe. The two others right behind them followed as well. If Alex thought that mark four was messy, then this was going to be a full traffic jam. He was sitting at the back of Dinghy. He had raised the centerboard and had moved his weight to the center of Dinghy's cockpit. He was also holding his breath and looking seriously concerned.

As they all descended upon mark five, the girl was leading and Alex was about even with the other boy and girl who had chosen the port tack route. But they were slightly closer to mark five than he.

Just when Alex thought he could squeeze them away from the mark, they began yelling, "ROOM - ROOM - ROOM!"

Dinghy then announced, "According to the rules Alex, we've got to give them room at the mark, unfortunately."

Alex bit his lip in despair. He'd thought that he could gain an advantage by going close to the mark and thus forcing the other two to miss it. But now, according to Dinghy, he'd have to go wide below the mark and let them through. Mark six was directly across the wind from mark five and off to the starboard. They'd all need to be on a beam reach immediately after mark five.

Although Alex had to give the two dinghies to the right room to pass the mark, he wasn't going to give them much. There were only inches between the boats as they speed around the mark.

Now, as they all came out of mark five, the girl was still leading with Alex and Dinghy right behind. The two other dinghies with one boy and one girl were directly abreast but upwind of Alex and Dinghy. Dinghy and Alex would have to make no mistakes. They had dropped back to fourth position now.

All Alex could do was sail the wind as best he could. Dinghy told him to push the centerboard all the way down and tighten the boom vang ever so slightly. While Alex couldn't feel it, Dinghy could. They increased speed ever so slightly. The two dinghies to windward were concentrating so much on Alex and the girl that they neglected to make their fine adjustments. The girl and Alex pulled slightly ahead.

Mark six was almost directly downwind of the finish line. After rounding that, the girl and Alex would have to go into a tacking dual to see who would win the race.

"Alex, when we come around mark six, our tactic will be to do the opposite of what she does. If she goes left we will go right. Unfortunately, if she is smart she will do what ever we do. If she wants to maintain the lead, she will need to catch the same wind as we do and the only way she can do that is to stay with us," theorized Dinghy. "If the wind is still veering, we'll want to go left. Let's hope she'll go right."

At the mark the girl played her cards thinking the wind was veering as well so she tightened up her mainsheet and stayed on a starboard tack but intently watching Alex to see what he would do. "We've got to go the other way," said Dinghy now hoping that the wind would hold steady or perhaps even swing back in a counterclockwise direction; backing instead of veering.

Alex tacked at the mark and went onto a port tack close haul. The girl hesitated but her training was good. She knew to cover the boat behind. She tacked over on to a port tack close haul as well. Dinghy now knew it was going to be a tacking dual, and the first to make a mistake would lose the race. He had confidence in Alex so Dinghy began directing him through a series of tacks to port and starboard. Each time the girl expertly covered. "She's like a robot," commented Dinghy.

About 100 meters short of the finish line, Alex and Dinghy had made no ground on the girl. They were on a port tack. The girl was also on a port tack, slightly upwind and ahead. The wind made a big change and produced a large knock turning both of them downwind. But this now also made the finish on a layline. If they tacked over, they could both sail directly to the finish line. The girl saw it too.

"Alex, pretend to get ready to tack but don't," whispered Dinghy.

Alex began looking around to see if there was clear traffic and readying the main sheet. The girl saw this and took it as a sign that Alex was about to tack. She tacked over and began laying in on the finish line.

"Hold your course Alex. The only way we can win this is if the wind lifts us back off this knock," said Dinghy. Alex detected a slight bit of anxiousness in Dinghy's voice.

And sure enough, a moment later the wind backed, lifting Alex and Dinghy back to their original course. The girl was still laying the finish line but it was the far end pin, not next to the committee boat like she had hoped. Alex and Dinghy held onto the port tack a little longer until the committee boat was on a layline. They tacked over to starboard.

Now it was a pure speed race and not a tacking dual anymore. The girl was way off to the left seemingly way ahead but going for the far pin end of the finish line. Alex and Dinghy were going for the Committee boat end.

"Race like you've never raced before!" Dinghy yelled out excitedly.

"I have never raced before," cried back Alex.

"Oh, well, ummm, then go hard Alex! Just go hard!"

Alex pulled tighter on the mainsheet, tighter on the boom vang.

"Lean out and further forward Alex. Think fat thoughts: hot dogs, hamburgers and fries, fish and chips - anything to increase your weight further out."

Alex shifted his weight and leaned out as far as he could, straining his stomach muscles and checking the telltales as often as possible.

The committee boat was getting closer, but so was the girl to the pin. It was going to be close, real close.

To make matters worse, the wind backed a little where the girl was and she instantly took advantage and expertly roll tacked her boat. It was a cool maneuver thought Alex. Dinghy whistled admiring the instant thinking of the girl. "She's good. Real good!"

About two meters before the line, Dinghy yelled for Alex to turn up into the wind. This brought Dinghy's bow up and over the line a split second earlier just like a sprinter bowing his head forward to get over the line in a sprinting race.

"BHRRRRRRP! BHRRRRRRP!" went two horns almost simultaneously.

Alex and the girl were both over the line, but who won? It was so close that neither Dinghy nor Alex could tell. It was all up to the committee boat now. Alex and Dinghy sailed over to the girl. She congratulated them on a great race, but she also did not know who won.

They both sailed back to the committee boat to ask them. The committee boat was busy blowing the horn for all the other dinghies crossing the finish line and writing down the sail numbers. When there was a break, both Alex and the girl asked simultaneously, "who won?"

An old man wearing a teeshirt that said Peter Blake Memorial Race Regatta, looked out of the boat laughing and said, "Honestly, none of us could tell. We've decided to give you both first place. Congratulations!"

Alex and the girl looked at each other. The girl was dark in complexion, and had beautiful wavy hair with a friendly inviting smile.

"What's your name?" asked Alex.

"I'm Alexandra," she said, "what's yours?"

"Alexandra, my name is Alex. I think this is the beginning of a beautiful friendship."

As if out of an old movie, an old DC-3 airplane zoomed overhead.

The both laughed and Dinghy began singing:

"Got out of town on a boat goin' to southern islands,
Sailing a reach before a followin' sea.
She was makin' for the trades on the outside,
And the downhill run to Papeete Bay."

THE END

Glossary

Aft
Towards the rear of the boat

Backing and Veering
When the wind changes direction it either backs or veers. If it changes to come from a direction that increases on a clock, for example, coming from nine o'clock to ten o'clock, then it is veering. If it changes to come from a direction that decreases on a clock, for example, coming from nine o'clock to eight o'clock, then it is backing.

Beam Reach
The direction that the boat is headed when pointed about 90 degrees from where the wind is coming. The wind seems to come from the side of the boat.

Bear Away
To turn in a direction away from where the wind is coming.

Boom
A horizontal tube where one end is attached to the mast via a flexible joint (a gooseneck). The bottom length of the mainsail is attached along the boom. The mainsheet attaches from the boat to the other end of the boom. The boom, in conjunction with the mainsheet, helps to adjust the mainsail angle to the wind.

Boom Vang
A set of lines and blocks (pulleys) attached at one end to the base of the mast. The other end attaches to about 1/4 of the way along the boom. Tightening the boom vang pulls the aft of the boom down which acts to tighten the leech of the sail. This decreases the twist out at the top aft of the sail and keeps more wind in the top of the sail. On windy days, the boom vang should be loosened to allow excessive wind to spill out the top of the sail which will decrease heeling angle.

Bow
The front area of the boat.

Broad Reach
The direction that the boat is headed when pointed about 120 degrees from where the wind is coming. Heading in a partial downwind direction.

Clew
The bottom aft (rear) corner of the sail.

Close Haul
The direction that the boat is headed when pointed about 30 degrees from where the wind is coming.

Close Reach
The direction that the boat is headed when pointed about 60 degrees from where the wind is coming.

Cockpit
The area where the sailor moves about in the boat.

Daggerboard
A board that slots down into the water in the center of the boat. It stops the boat from sliding sideways through the water.

Deep Broad Reach
The direction that the boat is headed when pointed about 150 degrees from where the wind is coming. Almost directly down wind.

Dinghy
A small sailboat. Typically in length of 8 feet (2.5 m) to 18 feet (5.5 m). Some have two sails, some have one.

Foot
The bottom edge of the sail. The mainsail foot runs along the boom.

Forestay
A wire running from the bow of the boat to near the top of the mast. It helps hold the mast up.

Gooseneck
The joint that attaches the boom to the mast.

Gunwhale
The outer top edge of the side of the boat.

Gybe (aka Jibe)
When you gybe boat, you turn the boat all the way through the wind so that the sail moves to the other side of the boat. The boat stern passes through the direction from where the wind is coming from. This can be a dangerous maneuver in high winds because the boom moves across very fast.

Head
To point the boat in a certain direction.
The top corner of the sail is also called the head.

Head Up
To turn the sailboat in a direction towards where the wind is coming.

Heading
The direction the boat is pointing.

Headsail or Jib
While not used on Dinghy's boat, a headsail, also known as a jib, is a triangular sail that attaches to a wire line, called a headstay, that runs from the front tip of the boat to near the top of the mast. The back bottom of the headsail attaches to the jibsheet (a rope) that runs back to the cockpit. The sailor controls the headsail angle to the wind by tightening or loosening the jibsheet.

Heeling
The boat is leaning over due to the pressure of the wind on the sails.

Hiking Strap
A strap mounted on the floor of the cockpit. The sailor hooks his feet under the hiking strap to lean out of the boat.

Hull
The boat itself. But just the boat. Does not include the rigging.

In Irons
A situation when your boat is pointed directly into the wind. It is not being powered by the wind.

Knots (speed)
A nautical term for speed. It is similar in speed to normal miles per hour but is about 15% greater. For example 10 knots is about 11.5 miles per hour. Also, 10 knots is almost 20 km/hr (18.5).

Layline
An imaginary line that runs outwards from the mark or buoy at which you are attempting to go around. It is determined by the wind direction. If you sail on the layline you can make it around the mark with the most efficient set of the sail. An upwind layline will typically extend down-wind at and angle of 30 degrees or so from the mark.

Leech
The trailing edge of the sail.

Luff
The leading edge of the sail. The mainsail luff is next to the mast. The jib luff is attached to the forestay.
Also to luff the sail is to allow the sail to flap in the wind.

Luffing
The sail is said to be luffing when it or part of it is flapping in the wind. It usually means the sail is not pulled in enough to towards the center-line of the boat.

Mainsail
The mainsail is a triangular sail attached to the mast and the boom at the bottom. By changing the position of the boom, the sail angle to the wind changes.

Manisheet
A line or rope that attaches from the center of the cockpit to the end of the boom. It allows the boom to swing out when the mainsheet is loosened or pulls the boom in when the mainsheet is tightened.

Mast

The tall tube (spar) that stands up in the center of the boat. It holds up the sail.

Names of Parts

Each part of the boat has a name. Sometimes those names make no sense. Learn the names from this glossary.

Painter

A line attached to the front of the dinghy to pull or tow the dinghy.

Points of Sail
Each boat direction relative to the wind direction has a name.

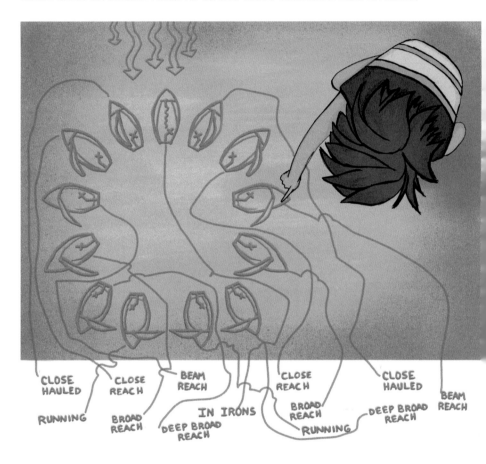

Regatta
A race or a series of races.

Rudder
A board at the back of the boat that is lowered down into the water. It helps steer the boat. The tiller is attached to the top of the rudder to help turn the rudder.

Run
The direction that the boat is headed when pointed directly or very close to downwind.

Sail Trim
To adjust the sails. Typically you adjust the sails so that they fly in the most efficient manner.

Stern
The back of the boat.

Tack
When you tack a boat, you turn the boat all the way through the wind so that the sail moves to the other side of the boat. The boat bow passes through the direction from where the wind is coming from. The bottom forward corner of the sail is also called the tack of the sail.

Tiller
An arm that attaches to the top of the rudder to help turn the rudder.

Tiller Extension
An arm that attaches to the top of the rudder to help turn the rudder.

Vang
A set of lines and blocks (pulleys) attached at one end to the base of the mast. The other end attaches to about 1/4 of the way along the boom. Tightening the boom vang pulls the aft of the boom down which acts to tighten the leech of the sail. This decreases the twist out at the top aft of the sail and keeps more wind in the top of the sail. On windy days, the boom vang should be loosened to allow excessive wind to spill out the top of the sail which will decrease heeling angle.

Veering and Backing
When the wind changes direction it either backs or veers. If it changes to come from a direction that increases on a clock, for example, com- ing from nine o'clock to ten o'clock, then it is veering. If it changes to come from a direction that decreases on a clock, for example, coming from nine o'clock to eight o'clock, then it is backing.

Test

Dinghy is testing Alex on the give way rules, names of parts of the boat, points of sail, and sail trim. Copy these pages and fill out the answers. The answers follow. NO PEAKING otherwise Dinghy will capsize you next time you are out.

Who Gives Way

Write in the box who gives way

Names of Parts

Write the following names in to the matching box

BOOM VANG   MAST   TILLER EXTENSION   HIKING STRAP

HULL   SAIL   RUDDER   TILLER   BOOM   MAIN SHEET

Points of Sail

Write in the name of the boat in the boxes
for each point of sail

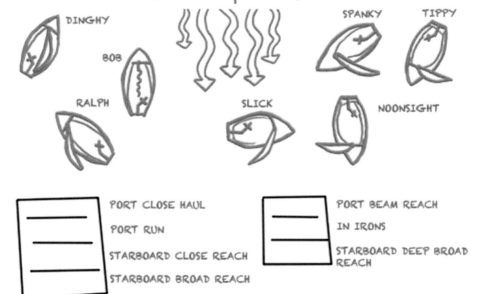

DINGHY

BOB

RALPH

SPANKY   TIPPY

SLICK

NOONSIGHT

_____	PORT CLOSE HAUL
_____	PORT RUN
_____	STARBOARD CLOSE REACH
_____	STARBOARD BROAD REACH

_____	PORT BEAM REACH
_____	IN IRONS
_____	STARBOARD DEEP BROAD REACH

Sail Trim

Circle the color of telltales
on Alex's side of the sail.

 Red   Green   Red   Green

Alex is on a close haul leaning
out of the boat. He sees the telltales
below. Draw lines to match two
correct actions for each view.

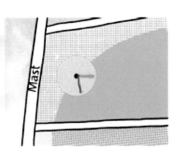

Boom Out
Boom in
Pull Tiller
Push Tiller

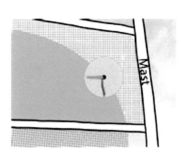

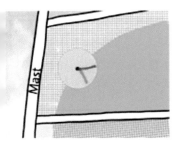

Boom Out
Boom in
Pull Tiller
Push Tiller

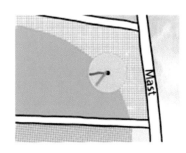

Answers

Giveway Rules

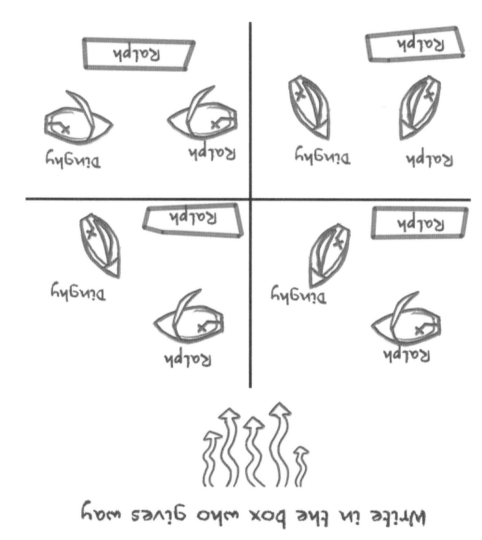

Write in the box who gives way

"Poor Ralph - haa haa"

Names of Parts

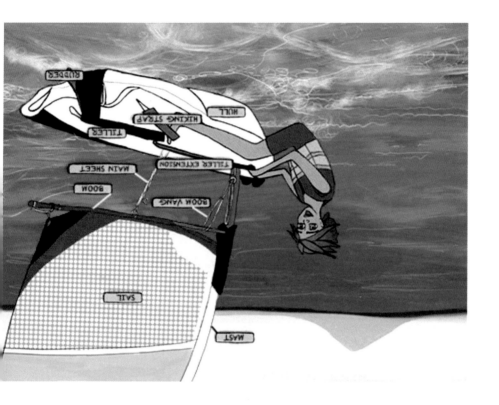

Write in the name of the boat in the boxes
for each point of sail

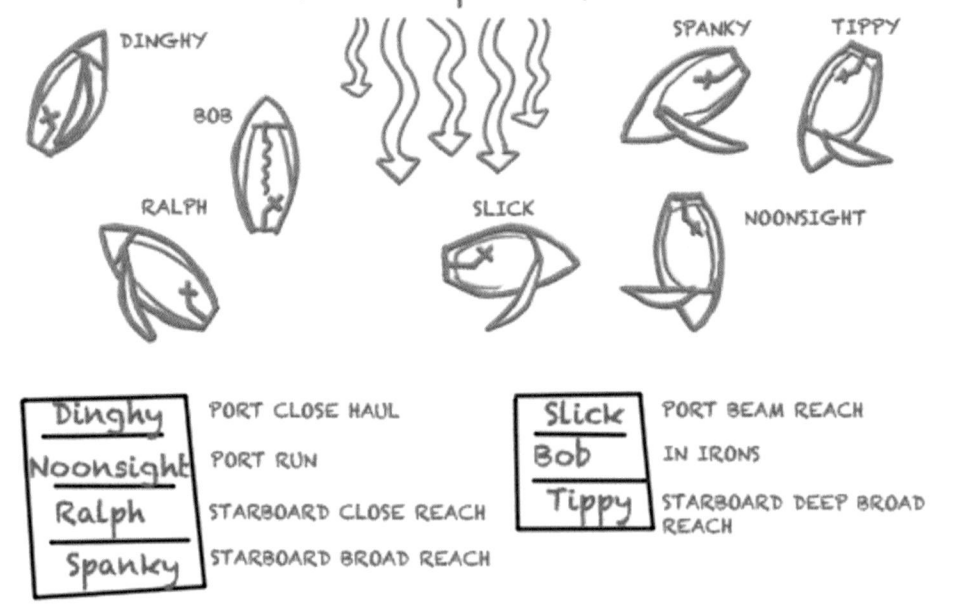

DINGHY

BOB

SPANKY   TIPPY

RALPH   SLICK   NOONSIGHT

Dinghy	PORT CLOSE HAUL
Noonsight	PORT RUN
Ralph	STARBOARD CLOSE REACH
Spanky	STARBOARD BROAD REACH

Slick	PORT BEAM REACH
Bob	IN IRONS
Tippy	STARBOARD DEEP BROAD REACH

Sail Trim

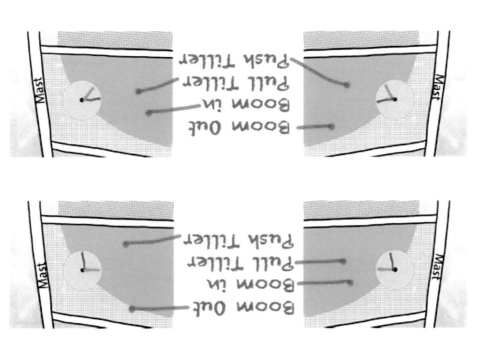

Alex is on a close haul leaning out of the boat. He sees the telltales below. Draw lines to match two correct actions for each view.

Boom Out
Boom in
Pull Tiller
Push Tiller

Mast

Boom Out
Boom in
Pull Tiller
Push Tiller

Mast

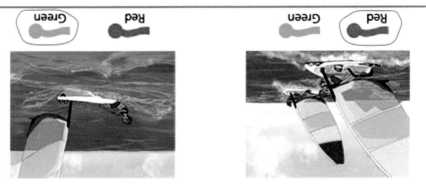

Red   Green   Red   Green

Circle the color of telltales on Alex's side of the sail.

About NauticEd

NauticEd (short for Nautical Education) is the gold standard for 21st century sailing education in both theory and practical on-the-water training. Sailing courses range from teaching to be a better sailor locally on a dinghy or small or large keelboat, to skippering a yacht on a sailing vacation, to sailing around the world.

Both the United States Coast Guard and NASBLA have officially awarded NauticEd with the following Verified Course.

Alex Learns to Sail is the second dinghy sailing training book to be released by NauticEd. The first being "Your First Weekend in Dinghy Sailing."

Whatever your sailing goals or desires, NauticEd has a full range of fun and interactive sailing courses as well as a large network of practical sailing training schools to suit.

Please enjoy all that NauticEd has to offer.

www.nauticed.org

Made in the USA
San Bernardino, CA
22 June 2020